Agnes grew up in the Western District of Victoria, Australia where, for five years, she created, produced, and directed children's literature festivals showcasing Australia's leading writers and illustrators. As a mother, Agnes dedicated time reading to her children from the day they were born, every day, several times a day.

Her passion for words combined with a sense of fun and rhyme has resulted in stories that children and adults will love to read time and time again!

A Prickle of Porcupines

Agnes O'Mahony

AUSTIN MACAULEY PUBLISHERS™

LONDON • CAMBRIDGE • NEW YORK • SHARJAH

A CIP catalogue record for this title is available from the British Library.

ISBN 9781398481640 (Paperback)
ISBN 9781398481657 (ePub e-book)

www.austinmacauley.com

First Published 2023
Austin Macauley Publishers Ltd®
1 Canada Square
Canary Wharf
London
E14 5AA

For Leah, Kirsty and Hugh.

Julianne (Epstein) Walsh's illustrations brought my words to life. Her faith in me, and ability to sketch what is dancing through my mind, is exemplary. Thank you Julianne.

A prickle of porcupines waddled down
the track

There were five in total from front
to back.

Three were on a mission to find a feast

Two were quite keen to get to the beach.

Along the rocky route they
found a tall tree

With limbs and large leaves,
close by the sea.

Branches heaved heavy with cherry-ripe berry

Perfect for making porcupines merry!

The thorny five snappily stopped
their search

With the tree and the sea,
it was the perfect perch.

They found a deep root, stuffed it galore

Then onward they shuffled
down to the shore.

Hedgie fished first to snuff out the scene

Followed by Quill who checked it was clean.

Barb did her best to catch a rough wave

While Needles and Spike avoided the shade.

Porcupines don't generally itch for a swim

They're usually seen sprawling
deep in the den.

But these five – ahhh, they were alive

They loved food and the ocean and
a big campfire!

The prickle of porcupines stood tall and upright

They planned to party and dance all night.

How happy they were in their hippy new haunt

Happy as hedgehogs on a nocturnal jaunt.

Ingram Content Group UK Ltd.
Milton Keynes UK
UKRC031034190323
418800UK00001B/1

9 781398 481640